BARNEY

Anthony Holcroft

Illustrated by Mark Wilson

Written by Anthony Holcroft
Illustrated by Mark Wilson
Designed by Peter Shaw

Published by Mimosa Publications Pty Ltd
PO Box 779, Hawthorn 3122, Australia
© 1995 Mimosa Publications Pty. Ltd.

Distributed in the United Kingdom by
Kingscourt Publishing Limited
PO Box 1427, London W6 9BR, England

Distributed in Australia by
Rigby Heinemann
(a division of Reed International Books Australia Pty Ltd)
22 Salmon Street, Port Melbourne, Victoria 3207

Distributed in New Zealand by
Shortland Publications Limited
2B Cawley Street, Ellerslie, Auckland

03 02 01 00 99 98
10 9 8 7 6 5 4 3
Printed in Hong Kong through Bookbuilders Ltd

ISBN 0 7327 1551 2

Contents

The Problem with Barney

Pete heard about Barney almost as soon as he arrived on the Tozer's farm. Old Barney had lived all his life in a small hut hidden away in the forest – and he lived there still. As Pete listened, he could see the hut in his imagination: the floor was carpeted with leaves, and vines clung to the crumbling walls. The wind and the rain blew in through empty windowframes.

"It's a wonder that the old man doesn't freeze out there," said Pete's uncle, Alan Tozer, who with his wife owned the land where Barney had his hut. "He should be in a home, where he'd have proper care."

But it seemed that Barney needed little more than the land itself could provide. Pete's Aunt Alice said that he knew the secret tracks of hare and rabbit like the lines on his hand, and he could point out plants that would cure you of a cold or the stomach-ache.

"Who would have thought the old rascal would live as long as he has?" said Alan Tozer. "You could have fooled me."

It was all of ten years ago that the Tozers had bought the big area of virgin forest. Before that it was owned by Barney's half-brother Marsden. It had never been farmed

6

or milled, and the heavily wooded land with its circle of swamp stood out like a ragged hedge from the neat crops and pasture land that surrounded it.

Alan told Pete that he sometimes felt annoyed just to look at it. "Good land going to waste," he grumbled. "And all that timber – there's a fortune in there!"

But when Alan had first tried to buy the land, Marsden hadn't wanted to sell. "The land's no use to me," he said. "But I have to look after my brother. What are you going to do with that land? Cut down the trees –

right? And then my brother, he'll be like a shell-fish without his shell."

But Alan had been determined. He raised his offer till it was almost double what the land was worth. In the end Marsden said he could have it, if he'd just get off his doorstep; but he also made a condition. For as long as Barney was alive, and chose to live on the land, no earth must be turned there, nor a tree felled.

"It's only right to protect my brother," said Marsden. "And I want your promise in writing. But when he dies, or goes away, then you can do what you like with it, Mr Tozer."

That was ten years ago; and Barney was still going strong, even though he couldn't be a day less than eighty. Once a month, in winter and summer, the old man wheeled his barrow a kilometre to the store; and then he wheeled it back again, heavy with supplies.

"I'm not a betting woman," said Alice Tozer, "but if Barney doesn't outlive the lot of us, I'll eat my hat."

Now it was the autumn and Pete had come to stay on the farm while his parents were overseas. Pete was a "loner", or that was the way Alan put it; a solitary sort of boy who enjoyed going off on his own to explore rather than riding on tractors or harvesters.

Pete knew the farm itself fairly well, but he'd never really thought about the forest that lay beyond. Now, more than anything, he wanted to see that mysterious Barney.

That evening Pete watched from his attic

window as the mists rose in the twilight. A sprinkling of stars appeared in the sky, but in the forest no light shone. Pete shivered to think that an old man lived in that darkness, in a tumbledown hut with no windows and no chimney.

He could imagine mist swirling through the empty windowframes, and frost slowly covering the bed like a stiff white blanket.

"But perhaps he doesn't feel the cold," said Pete aloud as he curled himself up in his warm bed, like a hare in its nest of grass.

The First Encounter

In the morning after breakfast Pete asked his aunt if he could visit Barney.

"I don't think you'll find him," she said. "He's shy as a rabbit with strangers. But if you must go, then make yourself useful and bring back some mushrooms. And be careful crossing that river. There's only a couple of planks, and they're as slippery as a skating rink. You'll need your boots."

Pete was soon setting out into the fresh autumn morning. Dew glistened on the tall grasses like beads of honey, and in the distance the forest cast a broad dark shadow on the fields. Above the tree-tops a hawk floated in the blue air.

It took Pete longer to reach the forest than he'd expected. He'd stopped on the way to pick mushrooms, and now the sun was well up in the sky.

Then suddenly the forest rose in front of him. The trees were older than any he had ever seen before. Light fell between them in dusty shafts, and there was a smell of spice in the air. The river flowed brown and silent.

Pete shivered, watching his breath drift mistily in the cold air. For a moment he wondered whether he should run back to the farm-house.

It was then that he saw the bridge. Not far from where he stood, almost hidden among the tall reeds, two thin planks spanned the river. They were still white with frost. Leaves were rustling in the wind, as if birds were hidden in the trees. It was a sound that made Pete uneasy. He held his breath as he crossed and tried not to look down at the river moving stealthily below.

On the other side a path led to a damp tunnel of trees. He stepped warily, like a cat through the forest, until he came to the edge of a clearing of tall, feathery grasses.

Standing at the far side was an old hut of crumbling, sun-bleached bricks. A sapling grew through the roof where the chimney should have been; a stone fireplace was outside the hut, and beside it, under a gnarled pear-tree, stood a rusty hand-pump.

Pete hooked his bag of mushrooms on the pump, and stepped cautiously on to the sagging verandah. Bees swarmed around a crack in the gaping doorway, and there was a warm, stale smell.

In the darkness something stirred like a bird rustling in a nest. Pete couldn't bring himself to look into the dark room. He leapt lightly off the verandah and ran across the grass and into the forest. He didn't once look behind him until he was across the bridge and safely in his uncle's open fields.

It was not until he was almost home that he remembered the bag of mushrooms on the pump. His aunt didn't want him to go back. "We can do without them tonight, and they won't be coming to any harm where they are."

"And there are some jobs to do here this afternoon," his uncle added.

But after breakfast next morning, Pete set off again. Once again he found the clearing. Some rabbit skins hung in the old pear-tree. This time Barney was sitting on the edge of the verandah.

"We've got a skink here, boy," he said slowly, pointing at something on a stone and then smiling up at Pete. "He lives under the stones and catches insects with that long tongue of his."

Pete went forward slowly and looked at the lizard.

The old man nodded. "Mokomoko," he said softly. "Come along, then." Barney opened his hand and the lizard jumped on to his palm and scuttled up his sleeve. Barney chuckled, and Pete saw that he had only two teeth in his mouth; one above and one below. His brown face was deeply lined, as though rain had made furrows in his cheek. But his eyes were sharp and bright, like a hawk's.

Pete felt a little shy. "I think I'll go now," he said.

Barney nodded. "Don't forget your bag, boy." It was hanging on the pump where he had left it. Pete thanked the old man and hurried home.

His aunt was really delighted with the mushrooms. "They look delicious," she said. "You've done well to pick such nice fresh ones." Pete looked too, and saw, not the big, coarse mushrooms he had gathered, but beautiful little button ones with the dew still on them. Barney must have picked them for him this morning.

Barney's Family

It was two days before Pete saw Barney again. He spent a whole day sifting through the ruins of the old flour mill, and most of the next afternoon assembling its treasures in his bedroom: an ancient coin, a bathtub leg, and fragments of coloured glass, their edges blunted by time.

That evening, he set out to see Barney. He found him picking pears from the old tree beside the hut. He nodded to Pete and handed him a basket. They picked side by side in silence. The dusky-brown pears were ripe, and slid easily into Pete's hands. On the side of the tree where the sun had been, they were warm to touch, like eggs in a nest. On the other side they were already cold.

Barney stored them in a barrel of sand for the winter. "No need to starve, boy," he said. "There's enough here for all my family."

"Where is your family, Barney?" asked Pete, puzzled. The old man waved a hand like a wand towards the forest, growing shadowy now in the twilight.

"My family is all around me," he said grinning. "Those big trees, boy. They're my family, and the birds that make their nests in their tops, and the insects that feed on their bark, and the river, and its fish, and the little springs that keep the forest cool in summer – it's a big family, boy."

"Will you show me your family, Barney?" said Pete.

"All in good time," said Barney, grinning. He reached up into the pear-tree and shook a branch. There was an answering flutter from the dark cluster of hens sitting in the branches.

"Time to roost, boy," said Barney. "Get off home now, and in the morning we'll see."

Pete sped like a hare through the trees and back across the bridge. Tiny night

moths fluttered up around his feet in the dusty grass, and behind him the forest blinked suddenly and grew dark.

In bed that night, Pete imagined the old man sleeping with his family all around him in the forest.

The next morning when he looked out of his window, Pete saw the forest, rising out of fields silvered with rain. Undaunted, he buttoned up his jacket, wriggled his feet into two pairs of socks and his boots, and set off.

At the bridge
he paused, and a
moment later he saw the
old man emerge from the forest.
He wore an old shirt tucked into his
baggy trousers, and a battered hat. He
looked pleased to see Pete. "To tell you
true, boy," he said, "I didn't think you'd be
coming."

He took Pete along the forest track,
showing him the trees and calling each by
name. He showed him shrubs, too, and tiny
scented herbs flowering under his feet. "This
is the pepper-tree," said Barney, as he bent
over a small bush with leaves blotched
scarlet and black, "but that isn't the name it
answers to." He made a clucking noise with
his tongue. "Horopito," he murmured. "Old
Barney wants a leaf."

Gently he plucked a leaf from the stalk and began chewing it between his two remaining teeth. "Good for the toothache," he grinned.

He offered a piece to Pete, but it made his tongue tingle, and he secretly spat it out.

"The trees – they're my family," said Barney. "I know every single one – I know them by sight, and I know them by feel. If I was blind now, I'd smell them out – I'm telling you true, boy. I know every one."

"My uncle says he'd like to cut your trees down," said Pete. "But you wouldn't let him, would you, Barney?" The old man grinned.

"Boy," he said softly, "your uncle is a man who thinks too much of money."

He plucked playfully at Pete's sleeve, squinting into his face. "Your uncle," said Barney, "if he opened his eyes, he would be dazzled by the land. Its spirit would move in him, and then – I'm telling you true – every tree would be sacred, and he would have to say a prayer before he cut one down."

"Is that what you do, Barney?" asked Pete. "Do you say a prayer to the tree?"

"I speak to the spirit of the forest," said the old man. "There is a secret place where the spirit listens and helps me when I am in trouble."

"Can I see the place?" asked Pete. But the old man shook his head. "First you must learn to know the forest and care for everything that lives there – you must become one of the family. And then you will find a secret place of your own." He patted Pete on the shoulder. "Tomorrow I'll show you some more of my family."

There was a scolding waiting for Pete at the farm-house. What would his parents say, his uncle wanted to know, when they returned home to find Pete in bed with the flu? But Pete's aunt wasn't concerned. "Don't fuss the boy," she said. "A drop of water never hurt anyone."

"Aunt Alice," asked Pete, when he brought his damp clothes downstairs, "do you and Uncle Alan really need that land?"

"*Need* it?" Alice thought for a moment. "Well, no, I don't suppose we do."

Pete's Secret Place

Luckily the morning was clear and blue when Pete set out. He had taken a picnic lunch, and now the whole day stretched deliciously before him. He found Barney making a pronged spear for catching eels at night.

The old man looked pleased when Pete came close, to watch. "Soon you'll be able to help old Barney hunt," he said.

But Pete was troubled. "How can you kill eels and hares when they're part of your family?"

Barney nodded. "I'll tell you true now," he said. "To hunt when the belly is empty is all right; and the eel sliding along the river-bed is a gift to the hungry belly. So is the hare

leaping through the grass.
One time I could pick off a hare
at a hundred metres – too true I
could. But the eyesight's gone bad this
last summer – it's not like it was. So you be
thankful, boy, for your own sharp eyes; and
just remember always to ask forgiveness for
taking the life of a creature, and give thanks
when your belly's full. It's like when you cut
down a tree, boy."

Pete opened his mouth to ask again about
the secret place where Barney spoke to the
spirit. But the old man shook his head.

"There's plenty of time, boy," he said. "Plenty of time. Why don't you go and find a place of your own, now – somewhere that feels right for you. Sit there for a while, and look, and listen; then come and tell me what you see and hear."

So Pete went into the forest to look for his own secret place. He walked at random, following first one animal track and then another, until presently the ground began to rise gently, and the trees grew smaller, and closer together.

Suddenly a great rock rose out of the forest. Grey lichens grew on it, and it

glistened with water trickling down its face. On the very top trees grew, and between their trunks the dusty sunlight sifted down. In a small mossy clearing at the base of the rock grew a kahikatea tree with big buttressed roots spreading out from the trunk like the arms of a chair.

Pete sat down against the trunk and rested his arm on one of the buttresses. It felt right for him. Then he shut his eyes and listened. The air was full of murmurs and crackling, and nearby he smelled the strong, ropy smell of one of the shrubs Barney had shown him. Something – a small bird, was it? – fluttered briefly near his cheek.

When he told Barney about the secret place he had found, the old man nodded. He told Pete that each day he must place his hand on the trunk of his tree to receive its blessing. "Do that night and morning," said Barney. "It will teach you to care."

So each day Pete went to his secret place. He rested his hand on the trunk of his tree until the rough bark felt warm and he listened and looked at the life going on in that small place; and afterwards he sat on the verandah with Barney and told him what he had seen that day.

Barney nodded gently, and once again Pete asked about the spirit of the forest.

"What does it look like, Barney?" he asked.

Barney shrugged. "It is like anything you think of," he said. "It can take many shapes. It may be a bird, or a flower, or a lizard, or even a leaf. You come to learn the signs."

He gave Pete's arm a friendly squeeze. "Don't be in such a hurry. There's plenty of time to see things. You're one of the family now – you really are." He chuckled. "One day," said Barney, "when I'm old and full of sawdust, you can come and look after us all! Our family, boy – it needs looking after."

The light in the clearing was beginning to fade. In the high tree-tops there was a small skirmish as birds settled down into their nests; and in the darkening sky the first stars had appeared like pale moths. "Get away home to your nest," said Barney. "There's another day tomorrow."

Pete raced home in the twilight. One day, he was thinking, when he left school, he'd save up his money and he'd buy Uncle Alan's farm. And then he'd be able to help Barney look after his forest; and he'd hunt for him, too. He couldn't wait to tell Barney his wonderful plan.

Trouble

The next morning, as Pete was slipping on his jacket in the porch, he felt a heavy hand on his shoulder. "If I remember rightly, young fella," said Uncle Alan, "we didn't finish that job down at the cattle yards – remember? Shouldn't take a minute."

But like all of Uncle Alan's little jobs, this one grew and grew until lunch-time. And then, after lunch, as he was trying to sneak away for a second time, his aunt appeared in the doorway.

"I want a word with you, Pete." As she spoke she pointed to the calendar hanging on the porch wall. "One week today," she said, "your parents will be coming to fetch you home. And what am I going to tell them about the homework you brought with you? There's no putting it off any longer; you'd better finish it today!"

It was no use arguing. It was clear that she meant what she said. Pete sat down at the kitchen table and stared blankly at the pages. He was worried about Barney.

"He'll be wondering why I didn't come today," he thought. "He'll think I don't care any more. He might even think I've gone home without bothering to say goodbye." There was nothing for it but to race through his homework so that he could get back to the old man and reassure him.

But Pete was a slow worker at the best of times, and trying to hurry was like being in one of those dreams where you're running and running, yet always on the same spot. Two whole days went by before his aunt and uncle would let him go out again.

Pete didn't want to take any chances. His plan was to slip through the fence behind the house; but to his dismay his uncle was there, re-straining a broken wire. "It's blowing up nor'west again," said Alan, glancing at the sky. "A good day for you and me to burn off that patch where the oats are going in. Shouldn't take a minute."

As usual, one job led to another, but by the middle of the afternoon Pete was free at last. The dusty earth smoked under his boots as he raced towards the river.

When he got to the clearing he heard coughing coming from the hut. He looked inside and saw Barney lying on his rough bed. His breathing was rapid, and beads of sweat stood on his face.

"Barney!" whispered Pete. But the old man didn't answer. He seemed to be asleep.

Pete ran back to tell his uncle. Alan was changing the oil in his tractor. He frowned as he listened to Pete. "What a time to get sick," he grumbled. "I want to get the barley headed while the nor'wester lasts, and then there's all this grass to cut. Still, I suppose I'll have to go." He threw down the oil-can and set off with Pete for the forest. When they reached the hut, Pete lagged behind his uncle, scared that the old man might have died. It was a relief to see him open his eyes.

"Hello there, Pop!" boomed Uncle Alan. "Couldn't see you for all the cobwebs. Your window's very clean though," he chuckled, punching a fist through the glassless frame. "So what's up with you, old soldier?"

"Just a touch of the flu," said Barney faintly. "I'll be right as rain."

Uncle Alan pulled a rough blanket up over the old man. "Of course you will!" he said cheerfully. "Keep warm and snug, that's the main thing. I'll send Pete back with some of our famous onion soup."

He winked at Pete as he stooped through the doorway. "I don't think it's anything too serious. The trouble with Barney is that he hasn't any friends, no tribe here, not even any close family. It gets to a fellow after a while." He saw Pete's anxious look and grinned.

"Don't worry, boy, he'll be all right. He's a tough old rooster. Though mind you, he shouldn't be roughing it on his own out there. At his age he could go out like a match."

He looked thoughtful. "I might get in touch with that niece of his – Mary or Marie, or whatever her name is. She should at least come to see him. It's not *all* our responsibility."

Pete had heard his aunt say that Barney had a relation who was a nurse. He hoped she would stay to look after him until he was better. "It's only a touch of flu," Pete told himself. "He's going to be as right as rain."

Uncle Alan seemed in a very sociable mood that evening when a neighbour called in. Drowsily Pete listened to the two men discussing the harvest. But then his heart missed a beat. "What do you think about that piece of forest, Jim?" Uncle Alan was saying. "Could you grow crops there?"

Jim nodded. "No problem, Alan." The two men sat silently for a moment, and then Jim said: "But I thought your hands were tied with the old man being there."

Uncle Alan leaned across the table. "I'm not taking any bets at this stage," he said confidentially, "but the old fellow might be going away. A bit of a holiday, you might say." He sounded pleased at the idea.

That night Pete tossed in bed, unable to sleep. The nor'west wind was blowing in through the windows, filling the room with a warm fragrance. He could hardly believe that his uncle really meant to get rid of the old man and cut down the trees. They offered a home to so many other living things, and they were ancient – they'd put down their roots in the land long before human eyes had looked upon it. Their smell was the smell of the earth, and their silence was filled with mystery. To cut them down would be to destroy more than just the trees. And what would happen to Barney?

He lay there imagining the roar of the bulldozer as it bit into the forest. He saw Barney's trees falling over one after the other and the sky rushing in to fill the gaps. He

tried to think of someone who could help Barney – someone who really cared. But there was no one.

"If I could do magic," he thought, "I could hide Barney's forest in a great cloud of mist when they come to chop it down; or I could put a shield around it to keep it from harm."

Pete closed his eyes tight and in his mind drew a white circle around the forest. It was a very big circle, including the trees, and the river, and the hawk that wheeled above it, and Barney lying in his ramshackle old hut; and before it was half done, he had fallen asleep.

Pete's Remedy

When he awoke in the morning, a high, unfamiliar voice floated up to him from the kitchen. Barney's niece Marie had arrived. He crept to the landing and peered down.

"Where's Uncle, then?" she asked.

"I'm afraid he's still living in the forest," said Pete's aunt. "And he still seems to love that old hut. Pete can take you to see him after breakfast. But you'll need to put on some boots. You won't get far in those light shoes of yours."

After breakfast they set out. Pete strode ahead silently while Marie trudged behind. "How much further is it?" she wanted to know.

They came to the bridge. She stared at it in horror. "How can I possibly cross that?" she said.

"Walk sideways," said Pete. "Like me." He went back and took her hand, and they shuffled slowly across.

They came to the hut. Marie stared in disbelief at the smoke-blackened clothes hanging from the rafters. "It's no better than a chicken-coop!" she declared. "All he needs is a perch." She stepped gingerly inside while Pete listened from the verandah.

She peered at the motionless figure on the bed. "Hi, Uncle!" she said brightly. "It's me – Marie! How are you feeling?"

Barney opened his eyes. "I'm all right," he murmured. "Right as rain." He closed his eyes again.

Marie felt his pulse. "You're going to be just fine, Uncle," she said, "but you'd be so much more comfortable in a nice warm place with someone to look after you. Just till you're feeling better. Just a little holiday, Uncle."

Barney cleared his throat. "Where's the boy?" he whispered.

Marie sighed. "Will you come home with me?"

"This is my home," said Barney.

Marie patted the old man's head. "Think about it, Uncle," she said. "Please."

She came out of the hut brushing her skirt. "He can't live in a place like this," she said to Pete. "I can't even see a stove where I could make him a warm drink. He should be in an old people's home where he could be looked after properly. At his age he's entitled to a few comforts, the poor old thing."

Pete glared at her. "Barney doesn't want to go away," he said. "This is his home. He has to stay here to look after the forest."

Marie sighed. "The forest will just have to look after itself, won't it? Things have to change. Now, are you going to give me a hand over this bridge?"

"No, I'm not!" shouted Pete, and he turned and ran back into the forest.

When he reached the hut he stood in the doorway, looking down at Barney. The old man appeared to be asleep. An empty sugarbag lay under the bed.

Pete took the sack into the forest and began quickly filling it with all the herbs that Barney had told him were good to use if you were sick: buds of young willow-green, "koromiko", and the inner bark of the tea-tree, gathered from the sunny side of the trunk as Barney had shown him. When the bag was full he took it back to the hut.

"Barney," he whispered, "I've brought some medicine and I'm going to set a fire in

the grate." Barney's eyes were open, but he made no sign.

"I'm putting the sack by your bed," said Pete. "There's firewood on the verandah."

Barney's eyes followed Pete's movements, but still he said nothing. Pete tiptoed out. He stood on the verandah, blinking in the sunlight. It was very still. Bees hummed in the shadows, and there was a warm smell of spice in the air. Never had the forest seemed so beautiful, and so frail. One puff, and it could all blow away like thistledown. He wished that he could capture it, in some way, like a landscape in a magic mirror.

"I must speak to the spirit," said Pete suddenly. He entered the forest, following secret paths until he came to his mossy clearing. He sat down under his tree, fitting himself snugly between its buttresses. Above him rose the rock, a dark core of stone older by far than the surrounding trees.

He shut his eyes. At once a picture of the rock began to form in his mind, a shadowy shape braided with glistening threads of light. He held the shape with his inner eye, and spoke to the spirit.

"Spirit of the forest," whispered Pete, "Barney is sick and needs help. I have given him some plants to make him better, but I am afraid that someone will come to take him away before he is well. And then there will be no one to look after the forest. The bulldozers will come and fell the trees, and turn the river into a ditch, and the fish will die, and the birds too, and the insects. Please, help Barney."

The shape of the rock in his mind had grown in clarity until he could see the lichen clinging to its silver surface, and the

young ferns sprouting from the crevices where the water trickled down.

And suddenly it seemed to Pete that he was standing on top of the rock, looking down on the ancient forest and the farmland

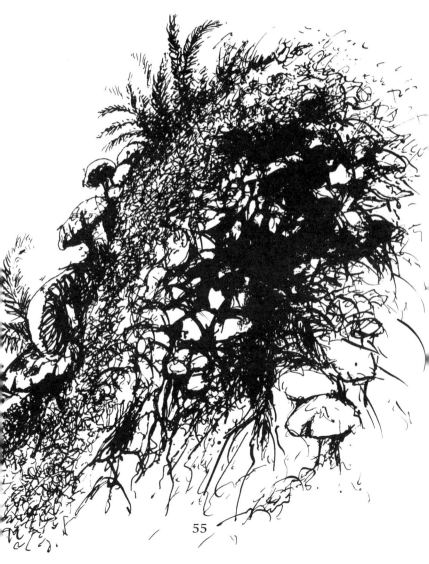

stretching away
beyond. Far below,
the river encircled the
forest like an island. It
flowed around and around, a
flashing circle of light, changing
colour; then it became as thick as
milk, darkening quickly to a murky-
brown colour, and moving faster. It made
him giddy to look at it. A sudden cold breath
rippled off the water, and Pete shivered. He
opened his eyes.

"Have I been awake or asleep?" he asked
himself. Above the great rock a hawk was
climbing into a darkening sky. It rose in
slowly-widening circles, like ripples in a pool

of air. A shadow passed over the clearing, and there was an unmistakable rumble of distant thunder. Pete jumped to his feet and ran.

As he burst out of the forest, the long grass crackled, and a cold wind whipped his legs. To the south, a solitary cottonwood tree behind the farmhouse gleamed ashen-white before the advancing storm cloud. Pete was racing in big leaps, reaching the back porch just as the first icy drops began to fall.

Moments later he stood with his forehead pressed to the window, watching a squall of rain drive across the land, and the forest vanishing behind it.

The Promise

Uncle Alan came roaring through the gate on his tractor. He stood at the wheel like a charioteer, water dripping from his face. "You wouldn't read about it!" he grumbled, as he kicked off his boots in the porch. "I never saw a storm come up so quick. Half an hour ago there wasn't a cloud in the sky."

But Pete, with his nose still pressed to the window, was elated.

"Flood, river, flood!" he whispered. "Then nobody can take Barney away."

But as the rain continued to rumble on the roof all through the afternoon and into the early evening, he began to feel anxious. What if the rain kept on and on, and Barney was swept away?

He imagined the hut swirling down the river like a sodden sparrow's nest, and shivered. If anything happened to the old man, it would be his fault. "I made the bad weather come," he said to himself, "by calling to the spirit for help." And now the rain didn't seem to know when to stop.

"Do you think it will be still raining tomorrow?" he asked his uncle.

Alan shook his head. "I wouldn't know," he said. "We often get storms at this time of year, but this one looks like being a bad one. I've never seen the river come up as fast as it has this time. It wouldn't surprise me if the bridge gets washed away!"

By morning the rain had eased to a light drizzle. When Pete looked out of his bedroom window, he discovered that overnight a lake had miraculously appeared. Beyond, the forest was afloat in mist, unreachable as a forest in a dream.

Marie was carrying her suitcase to the car. "I took two days off to come here," she said. "I'm sorry, but I can't stay any longer."

"Don't worry," said Uncle Alan cheerfully. "We'll fetch him over somehow, even if we have to hire a rowing boat. Then we'll post him to you."

By afternoon the water had gone down sufficiently for Uncle Alan to wade across the fields

in boots. He put on the heavy waders that he used in the winter, and set out to check the fences. Pete went with him, and his uncle piggy-backed him over the bad patches.

"The fences seem to be in order," said Alan as they approached the forest, "but I guess the bad news is still to come." And sure enough, when they reached the ridge and looked down, they saw that the bridge had been washed away.

A brown, frothing torrent swirled from bank to bank. A few flax plants rose above the water-line, and on the other side Pete could see a rivulet flowing into the forest where the track had been.

"There's no way of getting the old fellow out today," Pete's uncle said, "unless we bring in a helicopter or something. To tell the truth, I'm not sure what to do."

But Pete wasn't listening. He had sensed a movement, a stirring of the leaves; and there, like part of the forest itself, was Barney.

He stood at the edge of the dripping trees, knee-deep in water. His thick pants, tied at the waist with string, seemed to sag a little more than usual, but otherwise he looked as good as ever.

A frown passed quickly across Uncle Alan's face. "You could have fooled me," he muttered. He cupped his hands. "How are you, old-timer?" Barney's soft reply carried clearly to Pete across the roaring water.

"What's he say?" asked Uncle Alan.

"He says he's right as rain," said Pete.

It was Pete's turn to cup his hands. "Did you find the sack?" he shouted.

Barney's voice floated soft and clear as a whisper in Pete's ear. "I thought you'd gone, boy, without a goodbye to old Barney."

"But I left a sack for you," Pete called back, "full of herbs and things to make you better. Did you find them?"

Barney nodded. "I thought I saw you sitting beside me with a gift in your hand. It

was so clear, I woke up and thought: now where's that sack I saw in my dream? Then I felt around on the floor, and found it. And when I touched it my old numb fingers began to tingle, like when I put my hands on a tree – you know what I'm saying? And I was feeling strong enough to get up, so I brewed some herb tea. I'm right as rain, boy."

Uncle Alan was staring blankly across the river. "What was all that about?" he said grumpily. "I couldn't understand a word."

"He says he's right as rain," said Pete.

"He said that before," said Alan. He shook his head. "Tough old rooster." He began to move along the ridge, checking the fence.

Pete cupped his hands again. "I have to go home tomorrow," he called. Barney nodded.

"But I'll come back in the summer holidays. Are you really all right?" Now he came to think about it, the old man was definitely looking thinner.

Barney cleared his throat. "I told you, boy – I'm right as rain."

Uncle Alan had returned. "Come on," he said. "I've got work to do."

Pete turned to wave to Barney. But the old man had gone.

"Uncle Alan," said Pete, as they set off for home, "would you really cut Barney's forest down?"

His uncle gave him a playful jab in the shoulder. "Too right I would. One day I'll

have that place as smooth as a billiard table."

They waded on towards the farm. The water squelched in Pete's boots as he splashed through the shallows. "But it looks as though I'll have to wait a while yet," his uncle added.

Yes. Pete knew that, because of his uncle's promise, Barney would be safe so long as he kept well and wanted to stay in his forest home. Not even Barney's niece could change that, he hoped.

But Pete felt as though *he'd* made a promise too – to Barney and the forest. He'd have to make his parents understand. He'd have to come back and make his aunt and uncle understand. Pete thought about how the old man's hands had tingled when he touched the sack of herbs beside his bed. It made him feel that he *could* find a way.

Plans were already forming in Pete's mind as he threw off his boots on the porch and ran upstairs to pack. "Keep strong, Barney!" he whispered to himself. "Keep strong till I get back to you."

TITLES IN THE SERIES